It's the Great Pumpkin, Charlie Brown

 LITTLE SIMON

An imprint of Simon & Schuster Children's Publishing Division
1230 Avenue of the Americas, New York, New York 10020

Manufactured in the United States of America
First Edition 10 9 8 7 6 5 4 3 2 1
ISBN 0–689–84607–X

Adapted from the works of Charles M. Schulz

It's the Great Pumpkin, Charlie Brown™

By Charles M. Schulz
Adapted by Justine and Ron Fontes
Illustrated by Paige Braddock
Based on the television special produced by
Lee Mendelson and Bill Melendez

LITTLE SIMON

New York   London   Toronto   Sydney   Singapore

Dear Great Pumpkin,

I'm looking forward to seeing you on Halloween night. I hope you will bring me lots of presents. . . .

Every year Linus writes to the Great Pumpkin. And every year he waits in the most sincere pumpkin patch he can find, hoping to see his mysterious hero.

"On Halloween night the Great Pumpkin rises out of his pumpkin patch and flies through the air with his bag of toys for all the children," Linus explained to Charlie Brown.

"You must be crazy," Charlie Brown said.

Linus's sister, Lucy, cried, "Writing to the Great Pumpkin again? You'll make me the laughing stock of the neighborhood!"

Linus sighed. "There are three things I've learned never to discuss with people: religion, politics, and the Great Pumpkin."

Sally was the only one who didn't laugh at Linus. "You say the cutest things," she said.

"Would you like to join me in the pumpkin patch this year?" Linus asked.

Sally smiled. "Oh, I'd love to."

Linus was excited! This Halloween he would have company in the pumpkin patch. And surely this time the Great Pumpkin would appear! But first Linus had to mail his letter.

Nearby, Charlie Brown opened his own mailbox. For once, it wasn't empty.

"I got an invitation to a Halloween party!" Charlie Brown danced with joy. "I've never gotten a party invitation before."

"Is it Violet's party?" Lucy asked. "Your name must have wound up on the wrong list. You were on the *don't invite* list."

When Sally heard about the party she asked, "Is Linus taking me?" She wanted to go to the party, but she wanted to be with her "sweet baboo" even more.

"My blockhead brother is out in the pumpkin patch making his yearly fool of himself," Lucy grumbled.

"Boy, is he strange," Violet agreed. "Missing all the fun."

"Maybe there is a Great Pumpkin," Sally said, defending her sweetheart.

But Sally soon forgot about the Great Pumpkin. Everybody was getting ready for Halloween. All the kids were making ghost costumes, except Lucy.

"Where's Charlie Brown?" Schroeder wondered aloud.

"Here I am," Charlie Brown said from under a sheet full of holes. "I had a little trouble with the scissors."

Everyone recognized Pigpen by his cloud of dust. But there was one strange figure in the crowd.

"Who in the world is that?" Lucy asked when she saw Snoopy's costume.

"He's a World War I Flying Ace," Charlie Brown explained.

Flying Ace or no Flying Ace, Lucy decided to take charge. "All right. First we'll go trick-or-treating. Then we'll go to Violet's party," she declared as the World War I Ace slipped off into the night.

Linus was waiting at the pumpkin patch when the rest of the gang walked by.
"Have you come to sing pumpkin carols?" he asked.
"Blockhead! You're going to miss the fun again," Lucy said.
"Don't talk like that!" Linus exclaimed. "The Great Pumpkin will come because I am in the most sincere pumpkin patch."

"Oh, good grief!" Lucy marched off with the ghosts.
Sally went along. But at the last minute, she ran back.

Linus grinned. "You'll see the Great Pumpkin with your own eyes! The Great Pumpkin has to pick this patch. I don't see how a pumpkin patch could be more sincere than this."

Linus wasn't trick-or-treating, but he wasn't forgotten. "Can I have extra candy for my stupid brother?" Lucy demanded at each house. "He couldn't come with us because he's waiting for the Great Pumpkin."

"It's so embarrassing," Lucy sighed.

"I got a chocolate bar," Pigpen reported.

"I got a quarter!" Schroeder added.

"I got a rock," Charlie Brown said.

No one noticed that Snoopy was missing.

Snoopy had gone off by himself and climbed on top of his doghouse. He pretended it was a World War I airplane.

Ra-ta-ta-ta-ta-ta-tat!
The World War I Flying Ace fired his machine guns.
Ra-ta-ta-ta-ta-ta-tat!
The Red Baron fired back!
Curse you Red Baron!
The brave pilot went down with his plane.

The World War I Flying Ace sneaked off into the night behind enemy lines. He took shelter where he could, but always pressed on toward his goal.

On their way to Violet's house the gang stopped at the pumpkin patch. They couldn't believe Sally was going to miss the party.

"Just wait until the Great Pumpkin comes," Sally shouted. "Linus knows what he's doing. The Great Pumpkin will be here!"

But Sally was beginning to have her doubts. As soon as the other kids left, Sally turned to Linus and shouted, "All right, where is this Great Pumpkin?!"

While Sally and Linus scanned the dark, pumpkin-filled horizon . . .

. . . the rest of the gang enjoyed a great Halloween party. They bobbed for apples and played games for prizes.

There were caramel apples, popcorn balls, jazzy music, and spooky decorations. Everyone had a fantastic time!

Meanwhile, in the pumpkin patch, Sally sighed. "If anyone had told me I'd be waiting in a pumpkin patch on Halloween night, I'd have said they were crazy."

"Just think, Sally, when the Great Pumpkin rises out of the pumpkin patch, we'll be here to see him," Linus replied.

And just then there was a rustling in the nearby pumpkin vines! Could it be? Was the Great Pumpkin finally going to appear?

Linus saw a dark shape rise. His heart pounded. . . .

And then Linus fainted!

Sally took a closer look at the dark figure. It wasn't the Great Pumpkin. It was Snoopy! The World War I Flying Ace had found shelter in an enemy pumpkin patch.

When Linus finally opened his eyes, he asked, "What happened? Did I see him? Did the Great Pumpkin leave us toys?"

But there were no toys. There had been no Great Pumpkin—just Charlie Brown's dog, Snoopy.

Sally wailed, "I was robbed! Halloween is over and I missed it. You kept me waiting all night and all that came was a beagle! I'll sue!"

After the party the trick-or-treaters stopped by the pumpkin patch to check on Sally and Linus.
Sally was furious. But Linus still wasn't ready to give up.

"Hey, aren't you going to wait and greet the Great Pumpkin? It won't be long now!" Linus shouted.

The children just walked away. Sally left too.

"If the Great Pumpkin comes, I'll still put in a good word for you!" Linus called after them.

"Good grief, I said *if*, not *when!*" Linus cried.

"One little slip like that can cause the Great Pumpkin to pass you by," he said, fretting. "Oh, Great Pumpkin, where are you? . . ."

Ding-ding! Ding-ding! At four in the morning, Lucy's alarm clock chimed.

She got out of bed and went to Linus's room. As she expected, his bed was empty.

Lucy put on her coat and went to the pumpkin patch. She found her little brother shivering and alone. Once again, Linus had missed Halloween.

Lucy brought her brother home, took off his muddy shoes, and tucked him in bed. Another Halloween had come and gone—and the Great Pumpkin hadn't appeared.

The next day Charlie Brown tried to make Linus feel better. "Don't take it too hard. I've done a lot of stupid things in my life too."

"Waiting for the Great Pumpkin isn't stupid!" Linus replied. "Just wait until next year, Charlie Brown. You'll see. I'll find a pumpkin patch that's real sincere and I'll wait until the Great Pumpkin rises up . . ."

And who knows? Maybe next year . . .